"*The Wild Hunt* is Jane [...] ing herself by doing the seemingly impossible, creating a fantasy of Sort Of, Almost chapters that lead — Hold on to your helms! — into the landscapes of fantasy literature itself . . . *The Wild Hunt* will (guaranteed!) send readers of any and all ages scurrying back to that first Sort Of chapter to begin the wizardry all over again."

— Robert Cormier, author of
The Chocolate War and *I Am the Cheese*

"It IS original, it IS startling . . . I turned the pages as fast as I could from one Almost chapter to another."

— Anne McCaffrey, author of
the Dragonriders of Pern novels

"A work altogether unique and altogether universal. Jane Yolen gives us not only her own fresh vision of ancient mythology but, as well, she transforms these ancient dreams into something astonishingly new, immediate, and urgent."

—Lloyd Alexander, author of
Chronicles of Prydain

"Jane Yolen has taken some conventions of the genre that were getting somewhat shopworn and she has fashioned something that is simultaneously rich with old wisdom, yet shimmering with newness. What a triumph!"

— Bruce Coville, author of
My Teacher Is an Alien and *Oddly Enough*

"Steeped in mythology and folklore, this is Yolen's entry into the genre concerned with the origin of summer and winter, good and evil, light and dark. An intriguing chapter format . . . harks back to the uneasy boundaries between reality and perception much as they are in *Through the Looking Glass* . . . a complex, yet entertaining melding of a variety of European myths, legends, and folklore."

— *Booklist*

". . . a strange, haunting piece of fantasy. . . ."
— *Children's Literature*

"There is much power in Yolen's writing. . . ."
— *BCCB*

". . . evocative . . . dreamlike. . . ."
— *Kirkus Reviews*

"The language and writing are rich and precise . . . an attractive volume."

— *School Library Journal*

THE
WILD HUNT

THE
WILD HUNT

JANE YOLEN

Illustrated by Francisco Mora

SCHOLASTIC INC.
New York Toronto London Auckland Sydney

No part of this publication may be reproduced in whole or in part, or stored in a retrieval system, or transmitted in any form or by any means, electronic, mechanical, photocopying, recording, or otherwise, without written permission of the publisher. For information regarding permission, write to Harcourt Brace & Co., 6277 Sea Harbor Drive, Orlando, FL 32887.

ISBN 0-590-52836-X

Text copyright © 1995 by Jane Yolen.
Illustrations copyright © 1995 by Francisco Mora.
All rights reserved. Published by Scholastic Inc.,
555 Broadway, New York, NY 10012,
by arrangement with Harcourt Brace & Co.
POINT is a registered trademark of Scholastic Inc.

12 11 10 9 8 7 6 5 4 3 2 1   7 8 9/9 0 1 2/0

Printed in the U.S.A.   01

First Scholastic printing, March 1997

Much snow is falling, winds roar hollowly,
The owl hoots from the elder,
Fear in your heart cries to the loving-cup:
Sorrow to sorrow as the sparks fly upward.
The log groans and confesses
There is one story and one story only.

— ROBERT GRAVES,
   "To Juan at the Winter Solstice"

To Boiled in Lead,
who makes me dance and sing

I

CHAPTER ONE

Picture this: a great house surrounded by rowan trees, familiar and yet not quite. The house has chairs and tables and a library with bookcases that stretch to the ceiling filled with large books meant for grown-ups. It has beds in the upstairs bedrooms: three beds, three rooms. It has a bathtub with clawed feet and gold taps.

It has no radio, no television, and no locks on the doors.

CHAPTER ONE ∾ SORT OF

Picture this: a great house surrounded by rowan trees that are proof against magic. The house has a Grand Hall graced with floor-to-ceiling mullioned windows and a hearth in which a fire is always burning. It has beds upstairs in the bedrooms: three beds, three rooms. It has a kitchen with a walk-in pantry filled with canning jars packed with garden vegetables.

It has no radio, no television, and no locks on the door.

CHAPTER ONE ⚬⚬ ALMOST

Picture this: outside the great house, safely beyond the rowans, is a forest and a meadow and a world.

The forest and the meadow are full of dangers, some real, some imagined.

No one in the house is quite sure about the world.

2

CHAPTER TWO

A boy named Jerold lived all alone with just a cat in the great house surrounded by rowan trees. How he had come to that house, or when, Jerold did not know, but it does not matter. How and when are not what this story is about. It is about magic. Magic, the Wild Hunt, power, choices — and names. Only the cat understood that entirely. But cats always understand much more than they tell.

Jerold's story begins properly in winter. The snow had been falling steadily for most of the night and by morning was still coming down as if there was no end to it. The snowfall was very pleasant to watch if you did not have to be outside.

The house was silent. It was the kind of house that encouraged silences, with many carpeted rooms that seemed to unfold off long hallways. Most of the silences were companionable, but one or two of them — such as the dark, brooding silence of the basement — were quite unnerving. Jerold never went down there.

This winter day Jerold was in the library. He was most often in the library, reading books about wizards and sorcery, castles and kings. He liked those sorts of stories, though he did not really believe in them. Still, it comforted him to think that the world was laid out in easily identifiable chunks, this part light and good, this part dark and evil. In a great house filled with silences, such stories could be very soothing.

Jerold took down a big, heavy book from the third shelf and read it for about an hour without quite making out the point of it. The book was called *The Wild Hunt*, and it had very dark and realistic pictures of a man with a horned helm riding a horse, with a pack of slavering hounds and someone resembling a tree running by his side. The man, the horse, the hounds, and the tree person were all part of this Wild Hunt,

though who or what they were hunting was never made clear in the book.

Jerold didn't like the pictures and he didn't like the book either, but he couldn't quite put it away. So he sat there reading and occasionally putting his hand over the scariest of the pictures, though he felt as if he could still see them through the skin and bone of his hand. Unlike the other books he had read, this one had no comfort in it at all.

Suddenly a ball of white fluff seemed to flow toward the corbeled window. It resolved into a white cat who stepped daintily through a broken pane of glass, landing gracefully on the rug. There she sat down, silently licking between each claw, first her front feet and then, with a bit more difficulty but no less grace, her back.

By the time Jerold looked up from the book, the cat was thoroughly presentable. Jerold, of course, didn't care if she was tatty or tidy. The washing up was all the cat's idea. She stared at Jerold, her large yellow eyes both innocent and wise. Cats are like that.

"I have been walking up and down and to and fro upon the earth," the cat said.

"You found that in a book." Jerold's tone was accusatory. "Or in a story."

"Is it any less true because of that?" asked the cat.

Jerold didn't answer. Talking to the cat often made him cranky and his tongue sharp, and he found it best not to speak when his tongue turned into a knife. He could cut himself that way. He never seemed to be able to cut the cat. He suspected she did not bleed.

"Jerold," said the cat. "Jerold, I was walking up and down and to and fro upon the earth and I found tracks. Big tracks and little tracks and tracks of every kind. All jumbled together."

"And . . ." Jerold said cautiously, not daring to hope that they were, at last, going to have visitors. Any kind of visitors. He had been in the house for as long as he could remember and had never seen or talked to anyone but the cat.

"And — oh, you are such a *slow* boy sometimes." The cat gave her tail a quick but satisfactory lick. "And it means the Wild Hunt is once more on the ride."

"It means," Jerold said, this one time forgetting caution, "that you will forbid me to go outside. Or to let anyone in. It isn't fair!"

"If life were perfectly fair," the cat said dangerously, "you would be sitting naked under a twisted tree in a far-off country with other children. Starving. Instead of living here in comfort and ease with me."

Jerold had no answer to this since he did not know what the cat meant. He had no memory of any other children, save in the books he had read. He did not know what it meant to miss a meal. But he rarely understood the cat anyway.

"And," the cat continued, "I have warned you and warned you about the Wild Hunt." Her yellow eyes were suddenly fierce and like the amber they resembled, old and full of fossil information. "You have, I hope, finally read The Book? It won't tell you everything and — like most books — it will occasionally lie. But it will tell you something of the substance behind the shadows."

Jerold thought briefly about the pictures in the book: hunter and horse and hounds and tree. They were scary, but he knew they were not real. Only the house and the cat were real.

"You have told me stories," Jerold complained. "It isn't the same thing as information."

"Oh, but it is," the cat said, "if you know how to listen." Then she went back to licking her paws, which meant, Jerold knew from long experience, that the conversation was at an end.

CHAPTER TWO ∽ SORT OF

Now in that same house, but in a different time or perhaps in an alternate world — which is harder to explain than to understand — there lived another boy. He was somewhat like Jerold but not at all like him, too.

Outside this house the snow had also fallen for a night and into the day. But it was not a pleasant snow, for it was heavy and wet, bending the little trees and causing some of the bigger trees to break in two. There was a constant wuthering sound as the wind blew down from the north, edgy and biting, and the house groaned and griped in response. A fire roared, snapping and snarling in the hearth. In this boy's house silence was a scarce commodity.

"The Wild Hunt! The Wild Hunt!" the boy, Gerund, yelled, coming into the great room. And like the part of speech he was named after, Gerund entered running, falling, leaping, flopping, slipping, sliding, scrambling, tumbling along the dark wood floor. He was not a quiet boy.

There was a small white cat — just a leggy kitten, really — asleep by the hearth. The cat opened an eye, stretched herself awake, then moved deliberately out of Gerund's way. She had been in the house long enough to know him well.

"The Wild Hunt!" Gerund said again, pouncing on the cat and lifting her over his head, which she accepted with grudging graciousness. "Mully says it's come. Says he can smell it. Says it's riding the wind."

"Put me down," the cat said at last, and when Gerund had deposited her back on the hearth, she sniffed contemptuously. She really did not like being handled. And Mully was, after all, just a dog. What dogs knew came solely though their noses, a notoriously overrated instrument of knowledge.

At that moment Mully bounded into the room. He was a big, floppy dog, all ears-

17

over-eyes and a tail long enough for trouble. He had long, wet pouches on either side of his muzzle and gave slobbery kisses that took quite a time to dry. The cat tolerated him for Gerund's sake, but only just.

"I smelled it SMELLEDITSMELLED-ITSMELLEDIT!" Mully cried, exuberance overcoming diction. Like Gerund, Mully lived in exclamation points. The cat found this difficult to bear.

"You smelled something," the cat said slowly, "but as it is new snow, your nose is still adjusting to the exquisite tang of winter."

"I hate it when you talk like that," Gerund said. "Like a book."

"If you would read more often," the cat said, "or even at all, you would discover many truths therein."

"I discover truth in the wind THE-WINDTHEWINDTHEWIND!" howled Mully.

"You have wind at both ends," said the cat, "and the truth they reveal has more to do with your last meal than anything else." She stalked off into the next room, but before disappearing entirely, she looked over her shoulder. "Nevertheless, caution dictates that we all stay in for a while." Then she was gone.

"I knew she was going to say that!" Gerund exclaimed. "I knew we shouldn't have told her!"

"Oh, never mind, NEVERMINDNEVERMINDNEVERMIND!" Mully yapped. "Cats know nothing! They have retractable claws! We'll go anyway! Get your coat YOURCOATYOURCOAT!"

Gerund took his hat for good measure, pulling it way down over his ears, then slipped on his mittens, the good left one and the right one with the thumb that had come unraveled at the tip.

Then out into the snow and the wuthering wind they went together.

Chapter Two ∽ Almost

The riderless, mine-black horses blew whole storms out their nostrils. They pawed the snow away from the rock. Where their shoes struck the granite, bright sparks shot up. The sound was like a bell in a far-off church tolling the death of a man.

The hounds slavered around the horses' feet, muzzles brightly colored — magenta, cinnabar, vermilion, crimson, ruby, rose. They growled over their memories of the last hunt; they could almost taste time.

Nearby, a hairy Moss-man stood, as still as lichen. His dark skin, hard as maple rind, was brown and ridged, furrowed and scarred. Each feature of his face — nose, brow, lips — lay flattened against the scarring. He looked like the bark of a tree where a bough has been lopped off and the newer bark come up, overlapping the wound. His feet were bare but equally brown and hard. Running with the hounds would be no problem for him.

An owl flew on silent wings over the heads of the snorting horses, past the heads of the slavering hounds, in front of the brown-black eyes of the watching Moss-man, to land on the outstretched arm of an oak.

"Tu-hu," crooned the owl.

All — horses, dogs, Moss-man — looked up at the sound. The owl was a signal.

He is coming. The thought ran around the circle. *He is come.*

And suddenly, without further warning, a white horse whose outline was at once shrouded in fog and yet boldly stroked stood at the very top of the granite outcrop. On its back sat an enormous man, his black armor both polished and covered with a patina that spoke of centuries of wear. One hand rested on his hip; the other held aloft a long black whip. His horned helm was up, but if he had eyes, they were only red coals burning in the darkness that was his face.

With the hand that held the whip he snapped the helm down, and then the red-coal eyes were but embers behind the metal grate.

The black hounds suddenly leaped up one after another, crying out their obedience to their master, calling out their eagerness for the hunt.

The black horses, too, beat out their own eagerness onto the rocks, a swift, muffled tattoo.

And the Moss-man grunted his own willingness in a voice that creaked and moaned like a tree in a storm.

Its duty done, the owl flew off on silent wings.

"Halooooo!" roared the man in the black helm. "Awaaaaay!" His thunderous voice rolled.

Then, like a river crashing through rocks, the Wild Hunt began its terrible ride.

3

CHAPTER THREE

Jerold stared out the window, his mind jumbled. One part of him wanted to be bold and escape the cat's commands. The other saw terror behind the falling snow.

The pictures in the book he had just read suddenly came back with startling reality: the man in the helmet with its cruel horns, the horse the color of fog, the pack of hounds with their peculiarly colored muzzles, the ridged face of the tree-man. He thought he hadn't looked at them that closely, had covered them with his hand. But as if they had burned through his hand, had traveled up his arm, across his shoulder, up his neck and head and into his brain, he couldn't get them out of his mind.

"Cat," he whispered and suddenly, as if calling to her out loud had been a charm, the images in his head were gone. Relieved, he walked over to the window and looked out at the snow, white and steady. He traced his name on one of the windowpanes and watched as the frost outside outlined it in a shivery white.

"You should not have done that," the cat said. "Names have power."

"Is that why you have no name but Cat?" Jerold asked. He said it less out of curiosity than annoyance.

"I have a name," the cat said. "It is just that I choose not to reveal it."

"Well, I have been thinking of calling you Snowflake," Jerold said. He knew the very cuteness of the name would be a pricker-in-the-fur for the cat. "Snowy for short."

"Calling and coming are two different things," the white cat said. She stood and turned her back on Jerold, pointedly walking toward the door. Only the angry twisting of her tail gave her away. She paused ever so slightly at the jamb.

Suddenly Jerold wanted the cat to stay.

He feared the kind of silence that might enter the room if she left. "It's backwards anyway," he said.

"What is backwards?" The cat looked lazily over her shoulder, as if the question were of no importance whatsoever.

"My name," said Jerold. "From the outside it's backwards. It's only from *inside* that it's frontways."

The cat turned her head and deliberately walked into the dark and silence of the hall beyond. Only her answer returned to Jerold, in a whisper. "What makes you think it has any less power backwards?"

Jerold knew the cat meant him to think about that. Every syllable of it. And the awful thing was, he was going to think about it whether he wanted to or not. It was why the cat said such things. It was why she was so horribly annoying.

As he climbed the library ladder to put the book away, as high up on the top shelf as he could reach, far enough away so he couldn't get it down again easily, he thought: *Names. Forwards. Backwards.* Then, remembering all the books he had read where the heroes had at least two names — like Ged

Sparrowhawk, Aragorn Strider, Will Stanton, Arthur Pendragon — he wondered if Jerold was the only name he had. It was certainly the only one he knew of.

Outside, the snow kept falling. Softly. Silently.

CHAPTER THREE ～ SORT OF

They made slow progress. Gerund's foot-prints went humping, bumbling, slopping along. Mully's were great muddles and then a large white space, then another great muddle as he leaped up and over mounds of snow.

Gerund began to fall behind, and the dog called encouragement from somewhere ahead. "Keep going, KEEPGOINGKEEP-GOINGKEEPGOING!" his great voice belled. "Here's the way THEWAYTHE-WAY!" His voice seemed to fill all the spaces between the flakes.

Gerund caught sight of him, bounding and leaping. Then one great gathering of legs and a leap later, and Mully disappeared entirely behind a curtain of white.

"Mully!" Gerund cried, picking up his own pace. "Don't leave me. I'll get lost!" He followed the tolling of the dog's tongue. It rang out once more like a bell.

"Follow me FOLLOWMEFOLLOWME!"

"I'm trying!" Gerund yelled back, his voice cracking. Then, because he always knew he could call the dog back that way, he took off his right mitten and stuck two fingers in his mouth and whistled.

Behind them both, well out of sight but not out of hearing, came the white cat. "You certainly are that," she said, the words swallowed up and digested by the wind. "Trying."

The trio continued on for some time, heading — though only the white cat realized it — toward a granite outcrop about one hundred yards from the house. Soon the house, with its pretty sloping roof and mullioned two-story windows, was completely hidden from view.

The cat turned her head once to check that the house was gone, then silently — and not at all happily — trod on.

Bounding ahead, the dog was wet to the

bone, and Gerund, dodging and plodding along, was wet in layers. But the cat stepped alternately in Gerund and Mully's deep footprints and in this way kept her feet mostly dry.

Chapter Three ❧ Almost

The Hunt first went north, the greatest of the compass points, into the teeth of the storm. The Horned Man rode ahead on his great horse, and though his arrival at the rock had been sudden and silent, now he was completely a-jangle. Bells on the reins rang out, spurs clanked, armor creaked ominously; even the horse's hooves managed to strike low notes from the snowy path.

The troop of black riderless horses came next, a symphony of snorts and whinnies. A careful watcher would have noticed that the snow never fell completely on the horses. Though it hit flanks and withers, necks and heads, the snow somehow never fell on the saddles. An even more careful watcher would have seen that the flakes outlined what really sat on those steeds — riders as armored and helmeted as the master they followed, white as he was black. White riders invisible but for the falling white snow.

Accompanying them ran the hounds, sometimes ahead, sometimes behind, sometimes coursing on to the side and back again. Their bright muzzles shone like lanterns through the storm; they ran silently, for they had not yet spotted their prey.

Last of all came the Moss-man, who, of all of them, could keep up the pace night and day and never be winded.

The storm raved at them as they went north, then sang to them as they turned west, then laughed at them as they came south, then called to them as they moved east. There, at last, was the great house with its windows full of light, its sloping roof free of the snow that had slipped down to make soft piles around the walls.

The horses and hounds could not come close to the house. The rowans kept them at bay. But the Moss-man, being mostly tree himself, slipped through the magic barrier the rowans provided and came straight to the two-story windows. He sniffed first at the broken pane, then traced with a woody finger the fragments of name that still half shimmered backward on another. Then he bent over and traced with his own strong brown feet a series of odd footprints almost totally obscured by the falling snow. When he stood he lifted his right hand, pointing. He could see there was no lock on the door but, being a tree, he could not get in.

The Horned Man nodded. The hounds gave tongue. Then they plowed back into the ravening storm going north, back to where they had begun, the granite outpost a hundred meters from the house. There the hounds lay down in the snow breathing heavily, icicles bearding their bright muzzles. The horses once again pawed impatiently at the stone. Only the Moss-man was missing, having sniffed out a trail and told no one, not even his master, until he could check it out himself.

4

Chapter Four

Jerold looked longingly at the snow, then noticed a mess of footprints going to the right of the window. He tried to see them more clearly so he could figure out whose footprints they could be. They were certainly too big and too untidy for the cat, who was a dainty stepper. Yet she had told him often that the rowan trees would keep out anyone but the two of them.

He stood on tiptoe but still could not get the right angle to view the prints. So he turned and ran from the room and up the long stairs to his bedroom, which was almost — but not quite — above the great hall.

The neatly made bed stood a silent sentinel in the room. As he passed the bedside table, he smelled the familiar musty sweet smell of the potpourri in the blue willowware bowl. It was the only thing in the entire house that reminded him of summer.

Scrambling up onto the window seat, he stared down at the footprints. The falling snow had almost filled them in. From this height they were unreadable.

"Rats!" Jerold said.

"Be careful what you wish for," came the cat's soft voice behind him.

When he turned to look, she was sitting in the very center of the bed, a white shape on a white comforter.

"That wasn't a wish," he said.

"You would be surprised," the cat answered.

"I am," he said. "Always. At what you think."

"That is the best part of you," the cat said. "It's a sure sign of your innocence."

"I *know* that word," Jerold said. "Only I'm not really sure what it means."

"Innocence," the cat said again. "Guiltlessness. Sinlessness. Spotlessness."

Jerold looked down quickly at his hands, which were really not spotless at all, having got quite smudgy from the old book. He put his hands behind him and thought a single, silent, cranky thought at the cat. If it had been a dart, it would have drawn blood. Then he turned back and stared out of the window.

The footprints were gone altogether. He was filled, for just a moment, with something that felt a bit like sadness and a bit like dread, and a bit like nothing he could name at all.

CHAPTER FOUR ∽ SORT OF

Stumbling, Gerund followed the dog. Footprints and voices continued to encourage him. But after a few more minutes of staggering through the snow, he began to fear he was really going to get lost. He looked back over his shoulder at the house, surely only a few yards away, but everything was as solidly white behind as ahead. Putting two fingers in his mouth, he whistled a second time. When there was no answer, he cried out "Mully!" the name crumbling in his fear.

This time there came a long tolling of Mully's great voice. It went on and on, but faded as it went, until at last, with a final mournful note, it ran out.

Gerund was surrounded by a true and terrifying silence. What made it worse was that suddenly he could make no sound either, as if his voice had been tied, somehow, to Mully's; the one silenced, the other speechless. He kept opening his mouth, but no sound came out, only an exhalation of breath, made into white mist by the cold.

He spun round where he stood, hoping to find by instinct just which way to go. Looking down at the muddle of prints he and Mully had made, he was shocked to find that they had all been filled in by the snow. There was not even an indentation to show where they had been before. Ahead, behind, and on either side of him was a meadow of pure, unbroken, terrifying white.

"Mully," he mouthed in silence. The white mist spelled it out again. "Mully!"

As he stood staring out across the snow, a long, hard hand and arm reached through the whiteness and snatched him up, an arm and hand as brown as oak, as hard as bark. Though Gerund tried twisting and kicking, it did him no good. He was fetched up against something solid as a tree trunk.

When the tree blinked yellow eyes at him, Gerund found his voice at last.

"Help!" he cried. "Mully!" he cried. But he never called out for the cat, for he did not know she was out in the snow, and, besides, he did not know her name.

Chapter Four ∞ Almost

The Moss-man brought the kicking, squalling boy straight up to the granite outcrop and dropped him unceremoniously onto the rock. The sudden impact quite literally took Gerund's breath away and, for a moment, he could not do anything but concentrate on staying conscious.

"And what have we here?" came a voice from far above him, deep as sleep.

When Gerund looked up, he saw a man in armor towering over him. Or at least he saw the armor. He did not see the man. He also saw, and rather more closely than he wanted to, six slavering dogs. Unlike Mully, who was an ordinary brown and off-white hound, these were sod-colored dogs with fluorescent muzzles. They slavered and growled around him, and Gerund was afraid they were ready to bite. He backed up against the walking tree, which was as far as he was allowed to move. There were horses off to his right, and he did not like the looks of them either, for though they stood saddled and bridled, they were riderless.

"What is your name, boy?" thundered the armor above him. It was not a voice to argue with.

"Gerund," Gerund said, quickly adding, "sir!"

"I do not think so," the man said. At his words, the growls of the dogs increased. "That is not a boy's name. It is a part of speech."

"Please, sir, it is the only name I have."

"Then someone is playing a trick on you," said the armor.

For a moment Gerund remembered when the cat had told him his name. He had awakened on the floor of the great hall with no memory of who he was or how he had come there. He had gotten up and run around the house, jumping onto things and poking under things and slipping, sliding, and bumping about until he had tripped over the cat on the stairs.

"You are a walking gerund," the cat had said.

He had always supposed that was his name. Until now.

"Gerund," he said stubbornly.

The Moss-man lifted him up suddenly by the back of his jacket, high enough so that he was now looking straight into the helmet of the armored man, right into his eyes. Or at least into the red coals where eyes should have been. Gerund trembled in the Moss-man's wooden grip.

"Gerund," he repeated doggedly.

"I think rather . . ." the voice thundered through the helmet, "that I shall call you *Bait*. For I shall use you to catch the rest of them."

"The rest of them?" Gerund's voice squeaked alarmingly.

"The dog who should make up the seventh of my hounds," said the armored man. "For without the seven, the pack is incomplete. And Her."

"Her?" This time Gerund's puzzlement was genuine.

The helmeted man spoke, pausing between the names: "Albina. Io. Luna. Maia. Gaia. Cardea. Ravni."

"Please, sir," Gerund said, shivering uncontrollably now. "I don't know any girls. And certainly none by those names."

There was a moment of complete and unnerving silence. Then the armored man said, in a voice as hushed as death, "She is known in many nations by many names, boy. It is not surprising that you do not know them all. She is called also the Summer Queen, the Lady of Light, the White Goddess. Many names, but only one true name. If I can discover it, uncover it, recover it, She shall have to acknowledge me at last as the Master. But until I find out Her true name, we fight a battle at the year's turning. And Her champions die, one by one — as do my hounds. But whosoever dies, She still goes on. And so do I, my young Bait. So do I."

5

CHAPTER FIVE

Jerold walked out of the bedroom, point-edly ignoring the cat, who was once again cleaning herself thoroughly, as if she were making herself ready for some great moment. *A party or a christening or a confrontation,* Jerold thought. The last word was bulky and sat uncomfortably in his mouth. It was the kind of word he had only read and had never said out loud.

The long hall held a long silence; the stairs held a stepping silence. Jerold's footsteps were cushioned by the thick carpet. Sometimes Jerold thought he hated the silence, though he couldn't remember anything else.

As he came into the library, the silence

was suddenly broken by a loud howling outside, a bit like a dog but somehow worse than that, too. Jerold shivered and ran to look out the window.

In the snow sat the most unhappy creature he had ever seen, a hound of some sort, a slate-brown dog with patches like dirty snow. It was soaking wet and looked as if its face were running like candle wax, for its cheeks were wobbly, wet pouches, and its ears hung down well below its chin. About every thirty seconds it put its candle-wax face up and howled at the door. The sound was awful.

Jerold didn't know whether to put his fingers in his ears or let the pathetic animal in. He worried about wet paw prints on the carpets and the parquet floor. The cat would hate that. When she hated something Jerold did she went away for days at a time, leaving him to the silence. It was the worst possible punishment.

Briefly Jerold wondered if the hound belonged to the Wild Hunt, but it looked nothing like one of the slavering dogs in the book. Its muzzle was mud-colored and it looked as if slavering was not part of its vocabulary.

When the dog howled for a fourth and then a fifth and sixth and seventh time, Jerold made up his mind. Going to the door, he flung it open.

"Come on in," he called out, "but be quiet about it."

The dog shook itself thoroughly on the doorstep as if determined to leave all moisture outside. But it was solidly wet, having waded the equivalent of oceans to get to the house. It loped in crying. "I'm wet, so wet SOWETSOWETSOWET!"

"We hadn't noticed," the cat remarked dryly, entering from the door near the stairs. "Jerold, get a towel from the cupboard for Mully before he catches his death — and gives it to us."

Jerold was halfway to the cupboard when he realized the cat had known the dog's name. He wondered if that was important.

Chapter Five ∼ Sort of

The once bustling house was silent. There was not even a memory of Gerund's tumbling, stumbling, startling presence. It was as though a light had been switched off. Or a radio.

The snow kept falling in great wet flakes, like lace doilies soaked in water. The day trudged on toward evening. A hundred yards from the house on a granite outcrop might have been a thousand miles away. Or a thousand years.

CHAPTER FIVE ∽ ALMOST

It was dark when Gerund woke, shivering, shaking, and miserable. He was cold, but even worse, he hurt all over. His head hurt where he had hit it; his neck and shoulders ached from being hauled around by the tree man. And his stomach hurt just thinking about the hounds. It would have hurt worse if he had thought about the man in armor, but he didn't let himself dwell on that. Gerund was very good at *not* thinking about things that bothered him.

He was still on the stone outcrop, but it had changed somehow. It was no longer just a piece of rock in the middle of a great snowy meadow; it had metamorphosed while he lay sleeping. From the stone floor — still recognizable as granite — there had grown bars of stone, higher than he could possibly reach. However, there was no roof and the snow continued to fall upon him. Even the layers of clothes closest to his skin were now wet.

Gerund considered shinnying up the stone bars. But when he put his mittened hands on them, he felt the cold go straight through the wool, straight through the skin, all the way down to the bone. The bars were so cold they burned.

He snatched his hands away, whimpering. It was a small whimper, hardly audible. But it was enough. In answer, the hounds outside the cage gave off throaty chuckles.

"Gerund!" Gerund shouted at them, as if his name could silence them. "Gerund!"

The hounds were suddenly quiet.

Before Gerund could congratulate himself, a voice spoke from high above the bars.

"Awake at last, boy?" It was the armored man.

"Gerund," Gerund said again, only this

time it was in a very small voice, not quite a whisper, but close.

"Gerund or noun or verb or participle," the armored man said, "you are still but a boy. And a nameless boy at that."

Very slowly Gerund turned his face toward the sky. The armored man towered impossibly tall, glaring down with his red-coal eyes. Much to Gerund's surprise, he saw that the man's helmet had seven-tined horns, like a deer. It was not a comforting discovery.

"What possible use . . ." Gerund began, his voice cracking in all the wrong places. He started again. "What possible use can a nameless boy be to you?"

"Little stakes for big treasures," the horned man said, roaring with laughter. At the sound of it, the dogs all howled and the horses whinnied. There was little real pleasure in the sounds. Then a strange, windy tittering swept across the backs of the horses as if invisible riders were laughing as well.

Only the tree-man did not laugh. Though he had a mouth carved into his barky face, it did not open.

"She cannot resist trying to save Her champions," the horned man said. "Her trust in heroes will one day be Her downfall."

"I am no champion," Gerund said. "I don't even know what that means. And I am no hero. So no one is going to try to save

me. No one even knows I am here."

"The dog knows," said the horned man. "And where it goes, She will follow."

For a moment Gerund's misery lifted. *The dog knows,* he thought. *Mully knows.* Then, remembering Mully clearly, he was suddenly miserable all over again.

6

CHAPTER SIX

By the time the dog was dry, Jerold wasn't. Neither were the three large towels he had needed to complete the operation.

The dog dry was not any more prepossessing than the dog wet. He wasn't any quieter, either.

"I'm so dry SODRYSODRYSODRY!"

The cat shook her head in disgust. "In another time and in another place you will be a sports announcer," she said, "exclaiming on the already seen."

Jerold had no idea what she meant, but he suspected it wasn't a compliment. He took the wet towels over to the laundry chute and stuffed them in. He was heading up the stairs to change his own soaking shirt and pants when the cat called him back.

"We haven't time for that," she said. "We must listen to this windy excuse for a hound and plan our next move."

Jerold did not allow his puzzlement to show. Or his annoyance. He bit back a sharp answer and then let out a sigh, thinking about dry clothes.

The cat ignored him. "Now Mully," she warned, "say it truly and without the echo. Is the Hunt come?"

The dog shook himself all over. Towel lint flew into the air. "It has come HAS-COMEHASCOMEHAS . . ."

The cat rose and stretched her back upward, her tail looking like a spike of white mullein. Mully was suddenly silent.

"As I suspected. And where is Gerund?"

"Who is Ger . . . ?" Jerold began, but the cat turned her amber eyes on him and he fell as silent as the dog.

The cat looked back at Mully and nodded.

"The . . . tree . . . has . . . him." The dog spoke with extreme care, taking a breath between each syllable.

"Oh, Moss-man," the cat said, suddenly looking three or four times her size, "that thou darest go against me in this. I shall strip thy bark and make a boat of it to set across the river. I shall auger thy pith and marrow. I shall burn thy limbs in everlasting fire."

She sounded like a queen out of an old fairy tale. *And,* Jerold thought, *not the good queen, either.*

"Who *are* you?" he ventured at last.

"I . . ." the white cat said, looking straight at him and, as far as he could tell, all the

65

way down to his soul, "I am She Who Is Ever. She Whose Word Is Law. The Now and Future Queen. Maiden, Mother, Crone. I Am and Will Be, Summer and Goodness and Light." She smiled, but it was a cat's smile, sly and full of teeth.

"And *you*," Mully said in a low voice, "*you* thought she was just a cat."

CHAPTER SIX ～ SORT OF

Outside the now silent house the rowan trees rustled in the wind, as if holding a conversation. Their heads were crowned with snow and it made them look old and wise.

Two branches had broken off in the storm and lay one across the other on the path to the door. Over the door, from another storm's leavings, was tacked a third branch of rowan, almost obscuring what was carved into the lintel:

From creeping things that run in hedge bottoms,
Rowan, deliver us.

But the hedge bottoms were now filled in with snow, and whatever creeping things there were had long since been covered over. It was not creeping things the rowans protected against this night, but those that ran on four legs and two over the top of the crusted snow.

CHAPTER SIX ∾ ALMOST

The horned man walked away, leaving Gerund to his deep misery. Gerund didn't know whether to be frightened more of the man or the hounds. He suspected the man was a lot more dangerous.

Then Gerund wondered whether it was better to die a hero or a nameless boy.

Better not to die at all, he decided at last.

And finally, because he had nothing else to do, he paced his cage. The cage was long and narrow and reminded him of the great hall in the house, only made of stone. From one end to another it was 169 steps. Small steps. From side to side it was thirteen.

Gerund was not normally a quiet boy who took time to think, but here in his stone prison, thinking quietly was all he *could* do. So he took stock of his situation. He knew that the stone bars were unbreakable and that he could not dig his way out. There was also nothing to use as a lever or pry. He had a sudden memory of someone with a large flexible stick using it to leap over a high wall. It was not a real memory — not like his memories of Mully and the cat and the house. It was like a dream memory, as if from a time before he had been at the house. He had such dreams occasionally, though he never understood them. The cat would not talk about them, or explain.

He thought about making a rope of his clothes and knotting it around the top of one of the bars, but he realized that he had no way to fasten a knot high enough to do him any good. Besides, it was too cold to take his clothes off. And touching the bars burned his hands right through his mittens. He didn't want to even try to imagine what it would do to bare skin.

So he did the only thing possible under the circumstances. He sat down on the cold stone floor, wrapped his arms about his knees, and wept.

At first he cried quietly, because everything about the cage was quiet. But then habit overcame him and he cried out loud. The sounds came babbling, tumbling, waterfalling out of him. He did not care who heard.

7

CHAPTER SEVEN

Jerold looked thoughtfully at the two animals: the dog with his eager candle-wax face turned upward, the cat once again cleaning her paws as if she had never spoken. He wondered: If the cat were not a cat, could the dog be something else as well?

"Are you . . . ?" he asked Mully tentatively.

"Just a dog ADOGADOGADOG!" Mully said, his long primrose tongue suddenly slopping out between his jaws.

"A dog who talks," Jerold pointed out.

"*She* talks as well, Mully said. "ASWELL-ASWELLASWELL!"

"She doesn't so much talk as give orders," said Jerold.

The cat looked up from her paws. "When you two are through discussing the finer points of conversation, we can make our plans."

"Our plans for what?" Jerold asked.

"For GERUNDGERUNDGERUND!" Mully answered mournfully. "For the boy THEBOYTHE — "

The cat glared at him with her amber eyes and he stopped in midhowl.

"Isn't gerund a part of speech?" asked Jerold. "We studied that at . . ." He stopped talking as suddenly as the dog had, but not because of the cat's eyes. His memory had run out. He didn't know where he could have studied about gerunds. He couldn't remember ever being anywhere but the house.

The dog mumbled something.

"*What* did you say?" the cat asked, dangerously.

"I said . . ." Mully spoke softly, but there was a strange determination in his voice. "I said that Gerund is a tumbling, troubling, loving kind of boy OFBOYOFBOYOF-BOY!" It was the longest speech he had ever given.

"That's it!" Jerold said, rather more loudly than he had intended. "Gerund. It has something to do with . . ."

The cat shifted her gemlike gaze to him.

"To do with *ings*," he completed quietly. "Troubl-*ing*. Tumbl-*ing*. Lov-*ing*."

"The only *ing* I am interested in," the cat said in her precise way, "is rescu-*ing*. Which will work out most tragically if we do not make careful plans."

"Tragically for who?" asked Jerold.

"For *whom*," the cat said by way of an answer. "First we must go into the house."

Jerold bit back an even more ungrammatical reply and turned around and around in place till his body felt as dizzy as his mind. "I thought," he said, when the room had finally stopped spinning, "that we were *in* the house."

"The *other* house," said the cat.

"What other house?" asked Jerold. "Where is it?"

Mully leaped up, tail wagging like a metronome. "It is here ISHEREISHERE-ISHERE!" he belled.

"Where?" Jerold persisted.

But the cat had already started out

77

through the library door, the dog right behind. Afraid to be left, Jerold hurried after
them. When they reached the hall, it was
subtly changed. For one thing, there was no
carpet on the stairs. And for another . . .

CHAPTER SEVEN ∼ SORT OF

For another, it wasn't silent, like Jerold's house. He could hear the wind wuthering outside and the tree branches knocking against the windowpanes. The house shifted and creaked a lot, too, as if unable to quite stay on its foundations. Back in the room they had just left, Jerold could hear the sudden snap and roar of a fire that seemed determined to converse with the hearthstones.

"We are here," said the cat. "For once the dog is right. This may not be as quiet as the other for making plans, but it has more things with which to make them."

"I don't understand," said Jerold.

"Heroes rarely do," the cat said. She disappeared around the corner of the stairs, heading toward the basement.

Both Jerold and the dog hesitated following her there. It was as if they both agreed, even without saying so, that the basement was not a place for them.

Jerold sat down on the second step and Mully clambered up beside him, putting his big, floppy head in Jerold's lap. Without thinking, Jerold began to scratch the dog behind the ears and Mully shivered with delight, making little moans and groans that would have been embarrassing coming from anyone else. The house creaked noisily around them.

Jerold was surprised to find the sounds comforting. "Almost," he said aloud, "like a family."

Mully lifted his head from Jerold's lap and stared mournfully into the boy's eyes. "She is *nobody's* family," he said clearly. Then, as punctuation, he gave Jerold's face a large, sloppy lick, starting at the chin and traveling all the way up to the forehead with a single swipe of his tongue.

Jerold laughed out loud, a sound so alien to him that he laughed again.

Just then the cat returned. She was carrying something in her mouth that looked like a white mouse, until she dropped it at Jerold's feet. It had neither a head nor a tail.

"Take it," she said.

Jerold picked the thing up. It was white and slightly fuzzy and it was incredibly heavy. "What is it?"

"Ask rather what is *in* it," said the cat.

"All right: what is *in* it?" asked Jerold, using the cat's exact inflection. If he had hoped to annoy her, he was mistaken.

"Something all heroes need," the cat said.

Jerold waited.

"Armor."

"That's the second time you have called me a hero," Jerold pointed out. "But I am only a boy."

"What makes you think a boy cannot be a hero?" asked the cat. "Surely you have read about a few in all your books. Wasn't Ged a boy? And Arthur? And Will Stanton? Wasn't . . ."

Jerold glanced hastily back through the library door, where the fire had just snapped out a one-liner to the hearth. "What makes you think a boy *wants* to be a hero?" he asked carefully.

"All boys want to be heroes," said the cat.

"It is what they are bred for. Put it on."

"Put what on?" asked Jerold.

"The armor," the cat said. "It is time."

"It is time," Mully called, "ISTIME-ISTIMEISTIME!" His voice sounded remarkably like the funereal tolling of a large and ancient bell.

CHAPTER SEVEN ∞ ALMOST

In the stone cage the wet, cold, miserable boy slept again. He dreamed about hunting. In his dream he was not the hunter. He was the prey.

Outside the stone outcrop, the tree-man stood as if rooted, guarding the dreaming boy.

The six hounds lay at his feet, dreamless.

The horses with their invisible riders paced nervously around the granite. Their hooves packed the snow into a tight, white trail.

Of the horned man there was no sign. That was the greatest danger of all.

8

CHAPTER EIGHT

The silent house sat in the white drifts as if dreaming. Even the rowans in their magic circle were still. The snow no longer fell, but the air was filled with moisture, as if the storm had jelled into a kind of gray jam.

Slicing through that conserve rode the Horned Man. He came up to the circle of rowans, then rode around it, testing for a passage with his sword.

Poke.

Test.

Jab.

Test.

Thrust.

Test.

The rowans' magic held.

Angrily the Horned Man rode three times widdershins around the house, trying to unweave the webs that held it safe. But his sorcery consisted of brute strength and terror; neither served to sever the rowans from their hold.

Tilting his head back, the Horned Man screamed his fury into the stillness, then rode away. There was no wind to stop the cry, no magical barrier to its awful sound. It battered against the windows, shaking them. A small sliver of his anger found the broken pane the cat had used and, like a wisp of gray fog, crept through.

That was all.

It was enough.

Chapter Eight — Sort of

Jerold looked at the white box in his hand. He turned it this way and that. Although it was terrifically heavy, it fit comfortably in his palm. He could not imagine that it contained very much of anything, but especially not any kind of armor, which, he knew from his reading, was large and bulky and made of metal.

"Do it," the cat said.

"Do it DOITDOITDOIT!" tolled Mully.

Jerold looked again at the box. This time he saw there was a tiny gold latch on one side. He pried it up with his thumbnail and it opened with quite a satisfying *snick*.

"Well . . ." the cat said.

Jerold looked into the box. It was empty.

"Nothing there," he said, puzzled. He turned the box upside down and shook it as if to show her. Something white and gray and shimmering fell heavily to the ground.

"Put it on PUTITONPUTITON!" belled the dog.

Jerold stirred the thing with his foot. Though it looked as thin as a nightgown, it clanged solidly against his toe. He bent down and poked at it with his finger. It really *was* a kind of armor, metallic links all sewn together, with a cloth lining of some sort. He found what he guessed were the shoulders and held it up.

"White sammite," the cat said smugly. "Silken against your skin. With links of cold iron against the fey."

"You *are* the fey," Mully said so quietly that Jerold thought he was quite another dog entirely.

"I am a cat," the cat said. "Best remember that. Especially in battle."

"Battle?" Jerold asked.

"Put the armor on," the cat said. "And then we can discuss it."

Jerold took off his shirt and sweater and drew on the armor. The white sammite, whatever *that* was, felt smooth against his

skin. *Silken.* Just as the cat said it would. He could not feel the metal at all.

"Now you look a hero." The cat nodded, satisfied.

"I am a hero, too, HEROTOOHERO-TOOHEROTOO!" howled Mully.

"A hero," the cat said staring at the dog, "can be a sandwich as well. Mind you are not eaten."

"I am *not* a hero," Jerold said, certain he had said this before. "I am a boy. Just a boy." Then thinking better of it, he added, "A boy in armor."

"The best kind," said the cat. "Just be sure if you are captured you give neither your name nor mine."

"But I don't know your name," Jerold said.

"Yes," the cat said, "you do, though you are not aware of it yet."

Behind them, in the library, a whiff of the Horned Man's anger in the form of gray fog stiffened. It became a mouse-thing, mouse-silent, mouse-gray. It hid under the overstuffed chair and listened.

Chapter Eight ∽ Almost

The Horned Man's furious scream went around the house and to the four compass points.

South it hunted out a small badger wintering in its sett.

East it harried a fox along a path lined with oaks.

West it caused good folk in the village to test the shutters of their houses and bring in their pregnant ewes from the yard.

But north is where it went in its fullest fury, ravening about the stone cage. It woke the dozing dogs and disturbed the rooted tree-man. It made the horses toss their heads and stamp their feet in feverish fear. It entered into the dream of the sleeping boy, Gerund, and all the most horrible and irrational fears of childhood came tumbling in.

He dreamed of trolls as large as buses with fetid garlicky breath and teeth like tether stakes.

He dreamed of wolves beneath his bed and a great black bear in his closet, waiting.

He dreamed of guns and bombs and pocketknives and a familiar man on his street taking him by the hand and leading him into a dark unfamiliar place. And though none of these things was in the great house, in his dream he knew what they all were.

When the Horned Man returned, the boy awoke.

And he remembered his dreams.

— **9** —

CHAPTER Nine

In the silent house the gray fog-mouse could not see out of the library and into the hall, but it could hear the cat's voice. It knew that voice, knew it intimately over the years, over the centuries, throughout eternity.

The fog-mouse moved slowly toward the library door but still could not see out, for there was a kind of veil hung between the rooms.

It scurried silently back to the chair, back to the safety of the darkness under the chair. But it was not quick enough.

Something white, something fast, something deadly knifed through the veil and trapped the fog-mouse between sharp retractable claws.

The mouse tried to dissolve again into fog, into sound, but with a swipe of her paw, the cat swatted it across the rug and pounced again. The fog-mouse was silent through all this; the cat, on the other hand, emitted high little chuckles.

Then with one last slap of her paw, the cat sent the fog-mouse straight through the veil and into the hall.

CHAPTER NINE ∾ SORT OF

Mully and Jerold watched the cat leap over the doorjamb and disappear into the library, then moments later, something little and gray and silent came flying through the door, landing at Mully's feet.

The dog leaped on the gray thing and gobbled it up. He looked over at Jerold with an odd expression, part surprise, part delight, part fear.

"Bad dog!" Jerold said sharply. "Spit that out."

But Mully's expression changed immediately to something sly, something alien. He kept his mouth shut and, at the same time, closed his mournful eyes and swallowed.

Just then the cat walked back through the

door and cast its amber gaze around the hallway, somewhat — or so Jerold thought — like a lighthouse light searching through the vasty deep for wrecks.

"Where is the mouse?" asked the cat in a cold, tight voice.

Mully said nothing, his mouth firmly closed.

"Where is it?" the cat asked again.

Torn between the bounding good nature of the dog and his own long and odd association with the cat, Jerold was silent as well.

The cat drew herself up to her full bristling height and asked a third time. "Where . . . is . . . it?" There was no denying her now.

Jerold felt the answer leak out of his mouth before he could stop it. "The dog — Mully — he ate it. Whatever *it* was. I tried to get him to spit it out. I . . ."

The cat ignored Jerold's guilt and walked over to the dog. She put her paw almost carelessly on Mully's muzzle. He opened his jaws. Nothing dropped out.

"Oh, dog," the cat said, "your appetite has undone you. You have eaten a piece of winter, a piece of night, a piece of the dark."

Mully's tongue slipped out over his bottom teeth. It was no longer the color of spring primrose. It was as black as a cauldron and behind it his jaws gaped, deep and cold as death.

Chapter Nine ⟡ Almost

The Horned Man lifted his head and listened to the wind. He heard something the dogs did not, though their ears were very keen. He smelled something the Moss-man did not, though trees know the intimacies of every wind. He saw something the horses and riders did not, though they could see the grass growing. He knew something the boy in the cage did not, something beyond the realm of dreams. He knew about the mouse.

The Horned Man lifted his head and smiled. Not even his own Hunt took comfort in that smile.

10

CHAPTER TEN

The house was silent in its place and in its time.

The broken windowpane seemed etched with blood, the pane itself oddly opaque, as if the fog had slipped in between the layers of glass.

Outside, the wind silently puzzled through the rowan trees. The stripped limbs shivered once. Twice. Three times. Then they were still.

CHAPTER TEN ∽ SORT OF

Mully's candle-wax face seemed frozen. His tongue, the color of frostbite, seemed frozen as well. He said nothing.

The cat shook her head from side to side. "Ever thus," she said, and the silence after her statement was like a sigh. She shook herself all over. "Ever thus," she repeated.

"Ever thus what?" prompted Jerold.

Both cat and dog ignored him. He felt so silly then, standing in the strange-but-familiar house in a suit of sammite and metal, that he made a small movement as if to strip the armor off.

At once the cat stood. "It is time," she said.

"What about *making the plan?*" asked Jerold.

"The plan is awry," the cat said, almost whispering. "I had hoped this time it would be different."

"This time?"

The cat walked toward the door leading to the basement. "Come."

"I . . . hate . . . the . . . basement," Jerold said. "Can't we go out the front door?"

"This is the only way," the cat said. By way of comfort, she added, "The dog hates it, too." Then she went down the dark stairs.

As if giving the lie to the cat's assertion, Mully bounded after her, ahead of Jerold, his tail waving like a jaunty banner of war.

Reluctantly Jerold followed.

The stairs led down and down and down, farther even than Jerold had thought possible. The basement was windowless. There were no overhead lights. No candles in sconces, either. Yet Jerold found he could see well enough because the cat's white fur seemed to give off an odd light.

Cat and dog waited for him at the foot of the basement stairs.

"Pick me up!" demanded the cat, which was strange because she had rarely ever let Jerold touch her before.

Just as he was bending over, Jerold smelled something sweet and sharp and sour. "What is that?" he asked, straightening up.

"The river," the cat said, "where we start."

"Over the river THERIVERTHERIVER-THERIVER!" tolled Mully.

"What river?" Jerold asked, wondering how a river could flow in the basement without washing the house away. But before anyone could answer, he saw the river not a foot from him, dark and swift. "Why does it smell like that?"

"Taste it," Mully suggested slyly.

Since the cat said nothing against it, Jerold walked over to the river's edge, knelt down, and cupped his hands in the water. He brought them up to his mouth. He could see by the odd white light that the water was red. He stared at it for a long time.

"Blood?" he asked as last, though not really believing it could be true. It was only something he had read in an old book of ballads.

Mully lapped unselfconsciously at the river, but Jerold opened his hands and let the dark water patter back to its source.

"Blood," the cat confirmed. "Good you did not drink any."

"Blood," Jerold whispered to himself, trying to remember what happened to the hero in *that* particular ballad.

"Blood of heroes," the cat added.

"That's hardly any comfort," said Jerold, "seeing that you call *me* a hero."

"It is all the comfort you are going to get from me," the cat said, smiling her toothy smile.

Chapter Ten ❧ Almost

Gerund lifted his head and listened. First there had been the wind. Then the slavering sound of the dogs. Then something new.

What he heard was not the Horned Man's cry, for that was what had awakened him. He heard something he had not known in the house but had known somewhere else, beyond the realm of house and dreams. A rushing, pounding, tumbling, troubling sound.

The sound of a river in flood.

II

CHAPTER ELEVEN

The snow had stopped and above the silent house a pale moon, thin as a worn penny, rose over the trees.

The trees all stretched their branches upward, as if they were yearning to touch the moon or to draw some strength from it. But the moon ignored them and rose higher and higher still till it seemed to stop — or at least to hover — right above the stone outcrop that was a hundred yards from the house.

Then house, moon, trees, and sky made a sound together, like an exhalation of breath. Like a great sigh.

CHAPTER ELEVEN ∞ SORT OF

"Pick me up," the cat commanded again.

"Where is the boat?" Jerold asked as he bent to gather her up.

"What boat?"

Jerold hated when she did that, matching question for question. "Well, the one you were going to make from that whatchamacallit," he said.

The cat did not deign to reply.

"That Moss-man." He felt very daring to continue, with the cat's claws so close to his face. Maybe the armor *was* making him act the hero. Or the fool.

"In time," the cat said. It was not an answer. "In you go."

"In?"

"The river. Now."

Plunging into the river, the cat held firmly against his chest, Jerold felt the water lap his ankles like some sort of house pet. It was warm as bathwater.

Mully surged eagerly ahead.

"How far?" Jerold asked.

"To the other side," the cat answered.

The river bottom grew lower or the river water grew higher. It splashed against Jerold's knees, then his thighs. Forced by the rising river to swim, Mully paddled steadily across the red flood.

When Jerold looked down at the cat in his arms, her saw her white coat was flecked with dark spots. He did not, however, remark on it. Indeed, he didn't waste his breath speaking at all, needing it for the slog across the river. The water was waist-high now. It felt as if he were pushing through mud.

Suddenly he heard something, a sigh or a cry or a tolling bell. Belatedly he realized it was Mully.

"I made it MADEITMADEIT!" At the sound of Mully's voice, the river waters seemed to ebb, first below Jerold's thighs, then his knees, then ankles. When at last he could see the opposite bank, he hurried toward it gratefully.

"Put me down," the cat said the moment he reached the other side.

Jerold resisted the urge to drop her.

"Here," he said, setting her gently on the sloping bank.

The minute the cat's feet touched land, a light came on. Or rather, a pale moon appeared overhead.

"In the basement?" Jerold knew he had only *thought* the words, but suddenly they were loud enough to be heard.

"A hero," the cat said, "must go underground before emerging into the light of day. So it is written."

"Where is it written?" Jerold asked.

"In a book," the cat answered vaguely.

Jerold looked around. "This is hardly the light of day," he said sensibly. "That's the moon."

"No one said you have emerged yet," said the cat. "Listen to what I say, not to what you wish I had said."

"This is Faerie," tolled Mully, "where everything is widdershins WIDDERSHINS-WIDDERSHINSWIDDERSHINS!"

"*Widdershins?*" asked Jerold. It was a word

he had read but had never had explained.

"In a direction," the cat said, "opposite to the usual."

"To the usual what?" Jerold asked, not daring to hope for an answer.

As he expected, he got none.

CHAPTER ELEVEN ∽ ALMOST

Gerund stood up slowly. He ached every-where: hands, head, knees, ankles, feet. What didn't ache was cold, so cold it was like a red-hot heat. Above him the thin-penny moon sat as if unable to move away from the cage, as if it were caught as surely as Gerund by the stone bars.

Gerund gazed long and hard between the bars at the misty land. It was neither day nor night now but somewhere in between. The moon's wan light had turned everything into an overall gray.

Far off he thought he saw a river like a dark serpent, coiling and uncoiling.

Squinting, he managed to make out something — or was it someone — crossing the river. Someone lit by a halo of white light.

A hero? he thought. And then, without thinking, he cried out, "Help! Oh, help me. Please."

As if in answer, he heard the sudden familiar tolling of Mully's tongue.

12

CHAPTER TWELVE

All the lights in the silent house came on at once.

From the top shelf in the library a book tumbled silently to the carpeted floor and flopped open. The pages showed a battle between the Horned King's forces and a hero clothed in sammite and armor. The Horned King was winning.

The rowans outside stilled. And waited.

CHAPTER TWELVE ∾ SORT OF

Unlike his trousers and shoes, the sammite-and-metal coat was not wet. Jerold stood first on one foot, then the other, feeling uncomfortable and more than a little foolish. He didn't feel like a hero at all.

"Into the orchard," the cat said. "Quickly."

Jerold looked around at the gray landscape. "What orchard?"

No sooner had he framed the question than it was answered. In front of them a glorious walled garden suddenly appeared, the ground thick with wildflowers. Jerold followed the cat and dog through a gate and in front of them was the oddest orchard he had ever seen. Some of the trees in it were snow covered, some were budding, some were fully flowered, and the rest were over-laden with fruit. It was as if all the seasons of the year had crowded in together.

Mully bounced ahead to the part of the garden where trees fairly dripped fruit. "Time to eat TOEATTOEATTOEAT!" he cried.

Jerold was suddenly and undeniably hungry.

"Eat your fill YOURFILLYOURFILL!" howled Mully through a mouthful of fruit.

To his horror, Jerold realized that it was not an apple mushing through Mully's teeth but white worms. He turned for help from

the cat, but she was sitting cleaning herself again.

"That . . . that . . . fruit," Jerold stuttered.

The cat looked up at him, amber eyes in slits. "All the plagues in hell light on the fruit of this country," she said.

"Isn't that from . . . ?" he asked.

"A ballad," she said. "In a book. It is no less true because of it. All the plagues in hell *do* visit this garden. One's appetites must be controlled."

Jerold turned back to look again at the trees. What he had thought were snow and bud and flower and fruit were maggots and worms, aphids and flies. "Mully!" he cried out, but the dog ignored him and continued eating contentedly.

"Time, my hero," the cat said. She stood and walked past him, past the trees, over the carpet of wildflowers, and through a gate on the garden's far side.

Jerold took a deep breath and followed. And, after a while, so did the dog, his muzzle covered with something as white and wavy as foam.

CHAPTER TWELVE ⚬⚬ ALMOST

"Well done, little Bait," said the Horned
Man and laughed. The laughter crept in
through several of the stone bars, settling
coldly on Gerund's shoulders like a shawl.

The boy shivered violently but could not
dislodge it.

Uprooting himself, the Moss-man
clumped heavily to the Horned Man's side.

The hounds rose, slavering, to ring their
master round.

Only the horses were reined in, still waiting.

"Well done," the Horned Man repeated.
"It is begun at last."

Gerund did not like the sound of that at
all. For once, he actually would have pre-
ferred the silence.

13

CHAPTER THIRTEEN

House.
Trees.
Moon.
A shiver in the dark air.
A rip in the world's fabric.
It had, indeed, begun.

CHAPTER THIRTEEN ∾ SORT OF

The cat waited by a fork in the road where three paths converged.

The path on the left was narrow and rocky. Briar hedges lined the route, crowded so close together as to make the path all but impassable. Jerold ran his hand down the sammite-and-armor coat. He doubted even it could save him from those thorns.

The right-hand path was wide and inviting, winding lazily across a green glade. Mully was already bounding onto it, worms falling off his muzzle as he ran.

The middle path was not so well defined, for it went over bracken and fern. Here and there little bare circles of ground showed through, and an occasional hardy wildflower nodded in the slight breeze.

"Choose," the cat said.

Jerold guessed he was to take the most difficult path, the left one. Mully's way, the right-hand road marked with worms, was surely forbidden. But because he felt cranky, because he wanted to do something the cat did not approve of, he pointed to the middle path. "This one."

"Good point," said the cat. "But you are not a dog. You are a boy. Step on it."

Jerold did not move. "Where do the paths go?" he asked.

The cat's tail twitched in annoyance. "Paths go nowhere," she said. "People do."

Jerold bit back an answer.

Standing, the cat glared at him. "You are an annoying child. I don't know why I bother."

"I thought I was a hero," Jerold said. At that the cat looked startled. It made Jerold smile for the first time. He was still smiling when he stepped boldly — even, he thought, heroically — onto the middle path.

Chapter Thirteen ∾ Almost

Gerund waited.

The Horned Man waited.

The hounds waited.

The horses and their invisible riders waited.

Only the hairy Moss-man moved, like an oak in the wind. He turned his scarred brown face toward Gerund. His flattened lips tried to move, as if giving a warning. Or telling a fortune.

A dark, silent shadow flew across the moon, then settled on the Moss-man's out-stretched arm.

"*Tu-hu*," crooned the owl, as a boy and a dog galloped to the foot of the outcrop and stopped.

"Hello," Jerold said. He saw only another boy, shivering and unhappy, on a snow-covered rock.

Unaccountably, the dog stopped, sat down on his haunches, and howled. It was a sound like the end of the world.

14

CHAPTER FOURTEEN

The dog's howl filled the house, pushing every bit of silence into the corners, like dirt.

CHAPTER FOURTEEN ∞ SORT OF

The dog's howl filled the house, crowding out every other noise.

Chapter Fourteen ∽ Almost

"Who are you?" Jerold asked.

"Who are *you*?" Gerund answered.

The dog howled once again and the two boys turned on him. "Mully — shut up!" they said together.

"You know his name," Jerold said, wondering.

"He's my dog," said Gerund. "Of course I know his name." He put his mittened hands on the stone bars, heedless of the burning.

"He is *my* dog now," came a low voice. "Mully." And then there was a great cracking sound, like a whip. The boys looked up. Towering above them was a horned man. Mully cowered at his feet, muzzle reddening.

"He's bleeding," Jerold cried. "He's hurt." He reached out to touch Mully, but the dog growled, showing teeth the color and sharpness of steel.

"Mully!" Gerund cried. Tears started in his eyes and halfway down his cheeks turned into icicles. When Jerold reached through the stone bars and pulled hard at the icicles, they broke off in his hand. Where they had been, red spots like burns bloomed on Gerund's cheeks.

"I told you to be careful about names." A woman clothed in mist and crowned with elder leaves walked toward them. Her face was oddly whitened, as if with chalk dust. "Names have power," the woman said, but it was the cat's voice.

"You have come at last to my call," the Horned Man said, sketching a small bow.

"I always come," she said, with an abrupt curtsy. "But never when you call."

There was a great drum roll of hooves on the ground.

"My lady wife," the Horned Man said. "My queen."

"Husband mine," she answered. "And king."

"Master," he said.

"Never." She smiled. "So we meet again in the once-upon-a-time. What would you have?"

"Your name, your obedience, your loyalty." He held out his hand.

She moved closer but did not take his hand. Jerold saw that wherever she stepped, the white flowers of the trefoil sprang up.

The Horned King inclined his head slightly. "It is not easily that I get you to leave your starry castle there at the polar hinge of the universe to come to me."

"I did not come to you," the woman said. "I came for the boy. And the dog."

"The dog is mine already."

"Not completely," she said. Then she turned to Gerund. "Boy, how do you call him?"

"By his name?" Jerold guessed, but he knew they had done it already, to their great shame.

Gerund said nothing but whipped off his right mitten. Then sticking two cold fingers in his mouth, he blew a loud and long whistle. The dog didn't stir, but a wind began to puzzle through the winter trees, as if sniffing out its prey. The wind turned once around the outcrop, raising the hem of the lady's white dress. One of her feet was a woman's; the other was a cat's. The Horned King did not seem to notice.

Jerold turned to Gerund and whispered, "Blow again. Quickly."

Gerund blew a second time, and the wind raced swiftly over the rocky outcrop. It pulled at Gerund's cap, threatening to tear it from his head. Jerold felt the wind sigh into his ears and he clapped his hands over them.

"Again!" Jerold cried, but this time his voice was lost as an ear-shattering shriek of whistle and wind competed for the dog's attention.

Mully raised himself to his feet and stood, braced against the wind that battered him. Then he opened his mouth to howl into the wind and the wind scooped down his throat, choking him. He thrashed about, trying for breath, eyes popping.

"Mully?" Gerund cried, pulling at the burning bars with his hands

The other hounds howled the name back, as if mocking him. "Mullllllllly!"

Jerold couldn't stand it any longer. He flung himself on top of Mully, trying to shield him from the rest of the hammering wind. The wind beat upon Jerold's back, trying to shove its way through the metal links of the armor. It ripped at his hair, made ragged the bottoms of his trousers and shoes.

"Don't!" Jerold cried, heedless of his own peril. "Don't!" He cried it to the wind, to the Horned King, to the woman who had been the cat. "Don't hurt him. He's just a silly dog. Please."

He lay wrapped about Mully for what seemed like hours, until the dog grew first cool beneath him, then cold. At last the wind ceased and the only sound was someone crying. Jerold thought it was his own voice until he looked up. The crying came from the boy in the stone cage.

"It's not fair," Jerold whispered. "It's not fair *he* died. What did he ever do to deserve that?"

"It was his appetite," the woman said. "First the fog-mouse, then the blood of heroes, then the worms and wind. At least you kept him from the pack. What could be fairer than that?" She smiled at the Horned King. It was a beautiful smile but, like a cat's, had no warmth in it. "Game to me, I believe."

The Horned King bowed. "Your heroes, Lady, get younger at each turning."

She shrugged. "It is hard to purchase innocence today. Even childhood has been corrupted. That is the price of progress. I searched a long time for them."

"It is even harder," the Horned King replied, "to corrupt what is already decayed." He turned to the Moss-man. "Name the boy. You say you saw his script on the windowpane."

Jerold cringed, remembering, and held his breath.

The Moss-man's ridged face struggled to move. The flattened lips creaked with the effort. When at last that awful mouth opened to speak, it was as if it had been gashed apart by a woodsman's bloody ax.

"bloɪəʃ," came the ghastly voice.

Nothing happened. Jerold let a little bit of the breath he had been holding out.

"bloɪəʃ," the Moss-man said again. Then, exhausted by his speech, he closed his mouth. It seamed shut and he was suddenly rooted for good next to the outcrop, one limb poking through the stone bars.

"That is obviously not the right name," the woman said, her voice so casual only Jerold realized how nervous she was. "So you have no power over the boy. You lose the game and the set."

"But not yet the match," the Horned King said. Cracking his whip over the head of the pack, he cried, "Bring me the boy," and pointed at Jerold.

The pack surged forward toward him, bright muzzles flecked with froth.

"Quick!" Gerund called. He had managed

to climb up onto the Moss-man's limb and clambered out through the bars. Leaning down, he held out his hand to Jerold. "Grab hold."

Leaping as high as he could, Jerold grabbed Gerund's outstretched hand and scrambled up the side of the Moss-man's scarred trunk seconds before the pack reached them. Below, the hounds leaped and bayed uselessly.

The woman raised her hands, the finger-nails as white as pearl barley. "Enough, Lord Herne. There are two deaths between us already this year — dog and tree. It is enough."

"A draw then, my lady wife?"

"A draw then, my husband. Summer will again be but six months long."

"And winter the rest." Behind the helm the red-coal eyes seemed to smile.

She clapped her hands together and a fine mist rose, enclosing them. "Jerold," she said. "Gerund."

The power of their names called them to her effortlessly. Then mist and cold resolved itself into hearth and fire and rug and chair and they were home.

15

CHAPTER FiFTEEΠ

Jerold gazed into the fire, which finally had managed to penetrate to his bones, warming him against the cold. It was a quiet fire, made quieter by the fire curtain drawn between him and the logs.

He thought a long time about the difference between quiet and silence, between words and noise. Then he thought about the Queen of Light and the Hunter of Dark, how they professed to be so different and yet were the same. Finally he thought about choosing — and being chosen.

Heaving a deep sigh, he stood and walked through the door, calling out loudly as he did, "Gerund!"

CHAPTER FIFTEEN ～ SORT OF

Gerund was waiting by the uncarpeted stair. Well, perhaps *waiting* isn't the proper word, for he was fidgeting, scratching, picking at a scab on his cheek that covered a burn.

"Gerund!" Jerold called again.

"Ready!" Gerund said, though ready for what had not been discussed between them.

The white cat came daintily down the stairs. "Both of you?" she said. There was genuine surprise in her voice.

"It *wasn't* fair, you know," Gerund said abruptly. "About Mully, I mean."

Jerold was momentarily taken aback by Gerund's courage. Then he smiled.

"He disobeyed," the cat said. "His appetite . . . he would have been much worse off. . . ." For the first time the cat's voice seemed tentative.

"How do we know?" Jerold asked, genuinely puzzled. "How do we know that?"

"Know what?"

"That it would have been worse in the pack," said Gerund.

"Because it is *His* pack," the cat said. "Lord Herne's. The Horned King's. The Master of Winter's pack."

"That's it?" asked Jerold, anger rising. "Because it is *His* pack and not yours?" Jerold glanced over at Gerund, who had suddenly found the scab on his other cheek. "That's all of it?"

The cat sat down on the step and stared at the boys with her amber eyes. When she spoke again, her voice dripped with sarcasm. "Lord Herne is the dark, the night, the cold. He is chaos and anger and war. Of course it is worse in his pack, you stupid little boys. Now I . . ." and her voice quieted down to an enticing purr, "I have placed our dear Mully in the sky with Sirius, my dogstar. He will be ever so much happier there."

"Will he?" Gerund asked.

"Of course he will," the cat answered.

"Because," Jerold said, "you are light and day and summer? Because you are reason and calm and peace?"

"Because you are a bright little boy," said the cat, "and have read too many books."

"I thought," Jerold said dangerously, "that I was a stupid little boy. And the only books I have read were in *your* library."

The cat stood again and walked down the rest of the steps, across the hall to the door of the library. There she stopped and looked back at them, her eyes like yellow gems. "You are mortals," she said, as if that explained everything.

"It isn't good enough," Gerund said stubbornly. "About Mully."

Jerold thought a minute, then added, "Not in the *least* good enough."

The cat continued to stare at them.

Jerold went on, slowly, as if each word were a separate thought. "Mully didn't ask to be a hero. Neither did we."

"But he was," the cat said, going through the door. "He was *my* hero. And in the end, so were you. Isn't that what smart-stupid little boys want?"

Carefully Jerold took off the sammite-

and-armor coat. He was surprised how light he felt. How free. He put on a shirt and sweater. Then he called after the cat, "Mully isn't a hero. What Mully is — is dead."

"And what boys want," Gerund added, "is to go home. Though . . ." and for once his voice was low and thoughtful, "though I am not sure where that is, other than here."

The cat came back into the hall. "You *cannot* go," she said fiercely. "You are my Chosen, my Champions for the Year. You cannot leave until I dismiss you."

But the two boys were already gone.

Chapter Fifteen ~ Almost

They slammed the door and stepped onto the snowy walk. Behind them the quiet house and the noisy house faded. Hand in hand, they walked all the way through winter and into spring and on into the real world, somewhere, beyond.

Ms. Yolen's books have been translated into twelve languages and published around the world, and her stories and poems are included in many elementary and secondary school textbooks. Her song lyrics have been set to music by rock and roll groups and folksingers, and some of her fantasy stories have been made into animated movies.

A teacher, critic, professional storyteller, and lecturer, Ms. Yolen is married to Dr. David W. Stemple and is the mother of three grown children. She lives half the year in Hatfield, Massachusetts, and spends the other half in St. Andrews, Scotland, where she lives in a house not unlike the one in this novel.